even in our dreams

WILLOW WINTERS

Copyright © 2022, Willow Winters Publishing.

All rights reserved. willowwinterswrites.com

No part of this publication may be reproduced, stored in a retrieval system, or transmitted in any form or by any means, electronic, mechanical, photocopying, recording, scanning, or otherwise, without the prior written permission of the publisher, except in the case of brief quotations within critical reviews and otherwise as permitted by copyright law.

NOTE: This is a work of fiction.

Names, characters, places, and incidents are a product of the author's imagination.

Any resemblance to real life is purely coincidental. All characters in this story are 18 or older.

From *Wall Street Journal* Best Selling Author, Willow Winters comes a steamy, small-town romance.

Boy meets girl, boy falls for girl… but his friend asks her out first. That was back in high school and she was very much off limits.

A decade later, when he moves back to the small town they grew up in he's finally given his second chance. This time, he's taking it before she can slip through his fingers again.

This is book 2 of the Fall in Love Again series.

The Fall in Love Again series will feature Bennet and Bree falling in love on the small-town fictional street of Cedar Lane over and over again while the real world has had other plans for them. Because love is endless and this is what forever means. In any and every life, their love was meant to be. And there's so much to tell in the dreams where they get to meet again for the first time every night.

even in our dreams

Prologue

Bennet

Her rustling under the sheets is what keeps me from falling back to sleep. The bed groans slightly as the alarm goes off but I barely hear it. All I know is that last night was fucking incredible.

I'm in and out of it and as she hums, nudging her nose against my neck and whispers that it's time to wake up; all I can do is smile. There isn't a part of me that's ready to wake up.

It's a genuine pull against my lips as I grin and tell her, "Nope, I'm not waking up." Gripping the sheets, I pull them up and over the two of us, wrapping my arms around her as she squeals in protest. I turn to the side, holding her back against mine and smile wider as she laughs. All I can smell is her shampoo and the laundry detergent as she playfully objects.

"Bennet," she admonishes, although the laugh is still there, lingering in her gleeful tone, "it's time to wake up."

Kissing her hair, I ignore her. I keep my eyes closed and live in this moment between holding her and dreaming of her.

It almost doesn't feel real. She was the girl I couldn't stop thinking about in high school. The crush I never had the balls to ask out.

Fate brought her back to me a decade later and it all feels like it was meant to be. The other part of me knows it could all crumble so easily. We've only just fallen for one another.

There's so much at risk as she rubs against my arm, "wake up." She bats at me playfully. All the while I don't want to. I have the woman I've always wanted and a comfortable warm bed. I'd rather stay here and make use of the mattress like we did last night.

even in our *dreams*

"Only if it means I'll wake up with you in my arms," I joke with her, and she laughs that sweet sound.

"I'm right here," she tells me and then says, "You have to get going... before they find out you're seeing someone."

Like I said, it's all brand new. I wish we could just stay in this moment. Where she knows I want her and I know she wants me and nothing else matters.

Cause I'll be damned but I think I love her... I think I've always loved her.

chapter One

Aubrey

*L*ATE LATE LATE. WHY AM I ALWAYS TEN minutes late?

"Thank you so much for not canceling," I tell the nurse as she walks ahead and opens the door. "It's absolutely fine," Ginnie tells me. "We have a ten-minute grace period, but the new doctor is running late anyway."

"New doctor?" my eyebrow raises as the door squeaks shut and we're left in the privacy of a sterile examination room. The typical bed draped with that waxy thick paper and stool on wheels in front of a row of boring cabinets is all there is in the room. That and posters of skeletons and body parts that look like they belong in high school anatomy textbooks.

"Scale please," Ginnie chimes. She's one of my good friend's sisters and I nearly joke that I don't want to, but given how late I am, I toss my purse down on the patient bed and next are the keys, jingling as I drop them down too.

As I slip my tennis shoes off, Ginnie jokes, "You don't have to strip for this part." Her cherry red lips form a delighted grin and her chin length blonde curls bob as she chuckles at her own joke.

I laugh too, to be polite but also because the scale doesn't matter. Least as far as I know it doesn't. Today is just a checkup and I've always been around the same weight since high school. Well maybe five or ten pounds over, but I don't have to update it on my I.D. and that extra weight is to be expected… since wine exists.

As she taps the little weights to get my weight, I ask her, "You said there's a new doctor?

"Oh yeah. And new to town," she purses her lips after mumbling my weight while writing it down on

even in our *dreams*

my chart on the clipboard. Once she's done, she holds it to her chest and sways. "He's a hottie too."

She gestures to the bed and I toss my keys in my purse then put my purse on my lap as I take my seat. I practically hug it as I wait for what's next. It's been a bit since I've been to the Doctors. I probably wouldn't have even known this hottie doctor was new.

Ginnie is younger by about five years my senior. We didn't grow up together really since Lauren and I were always enrolled in a grade school ahead of her, but that doesn't mean I haven't heard all about Ginnie's dating life. I can only nod as she describes the new doctor and I recount the number of stories Marlena has told me with a bottle of wine in one hand and her phone in the other, texting Ginnie to keep her out of trouble.

"You know my cousin asked him out," she tells me, before setting down the clipboard on the counter and pulling down the top of her blue scrubs as she sits. "Arm out," she commands as she drags out a blood pressure cuff from a drawer. "He said no and I haven't a clue why. They would make cute babies."

She continues rambling as she gets her stethoscope in place. "Good looking doctor, no reason why he should be single."

I almost give a comment that maybe he's secretly dating someone or has a long-distance relationship since he's new to town, but she looks up to the ceiling, obviously attempting to listen to my pulse.

She whispers under her breath before jotting down the numbers on my chart and clicking the end of the pen as she searches the sheet for any missing information.

Before I can comment, she peers up at me, those blue eyes so very full of naivety, "Well you're cute— how about you ask him out?"

I can't help the grin as I huff a laugh and wave her off. "Me? Oh, no. Me and my lonesome are just fine." I have my books coming day in and day out as I edit them and an easy carefree life. I've tried dating and it just … it has not happened. "Dating almost always ends in disaster for me," I admit. In fact, I can't remember the last time I was excited for a second date. Or the last time I've felt attracted enough for a third date. Until this moment I hadn't realized, it's been almost two years since I've been intimate with a man. My gaze lowers to my purse which is sitting on top of the location I just thought might have cobwebs.

"A lonely heart isn't something to ignore," Nurse Ginnie tells me with a tone that reflects wisdom…

even if the mouth it's coming out of lacks that when it comes to men.

Still, she catches me off guard.

With my lips parted to respond, she cuts me off, "Just undress and put this on." With a wink, she passes me the thick pastel blue fabric sheet, "And then doctor hottie will join you." She chuckles again as she leaves and all I do is thank her, pushing down the anxious butterflies that have been asleep forever, but are not disturbed.

I recall every bad date I've had since college as I strip, folding my clothes and setting them on the bed. The back half is raised so they have to lay where my bottom just was. It was one bad date after the other. Somehow each one worse than the last.

At that thought, I realize the sheet dressing she gave me must be upside down or backwards. In nothing but my underwear and a sheet, I cluck my tongue, trying to figure this thing out. Why can't they make it easy like a robe? There are a couple of snaps and ties and I attempt to get it right as the memories flood me.

From bad breath kisses, to being cat fished and stood up.

There's only so much a girl can take.

I fiddle with the ties, attempting to get it tight,

but decide on leaving them be. I'm covered and I'm pretty sure it's on correctly. With that settled, I lift the pile of clothes and my heavy purse on top.

My feet dangle off the edge and I let them sway, until I remember the last date I went on and how I swore I would never do a blind date again. Mark was an ass. That statement is so true, I nearly say it out loud. As my gaze searches the small room, I see another stool, tucked to the right of the bed. I'm busying trying to balance the clothes while kicking out the stool when the doctor's voice comes through the door.

"Knock, knock. All set?" he asks and my heart stops. I swear I know that voice.

"All set," I call out and drop the clothes and purse to the new stool beside me. Only the purse is heavy and snagged on the pastel sheet covering me, pulling it down with me and the moment that door opens, it plays in slow motion.

My keys falling out of my purse and clinking to the floor, my hand going up as I yell out, "wait!" as the sheet that's supposed to cover me slips down. Embarrassment floods my cheeks with heat that must've come directly from the sun.

And my crush from high school, with his

gorgeous eyes widening, comes in and stares right at my naked left boob, soft nipple and all, that peeks out from the sheet covering I couldn't figure out how to tie.

Oh, my God, no.

chapter Two

Bennet

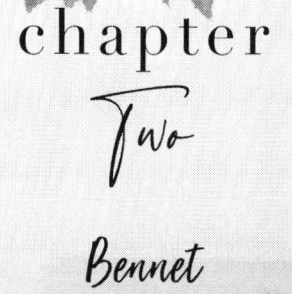

"Oh my God, out!" her shriek is clearly heard and yet I hesitate just a second too long.

As I turn, realizing, I'm staring into the mortified face of a woman I can't believe is even here, my back hits the door, my hand misses the knob and I nearly smack my face against the edge of the door before somehow managing to get the hell out of the room.

Wide eyes from Ginnie meet mine as she pauses

in the hall. I wave her off with the clipboard in my hand, pretending that my heart isn't racing. That it isn't attempting to gallop out of my chest.

"I'm sorry, all good now!" her feminine voice calls from beyond the door.

Composure. Composure. It takes two deep breaths for me to grab the door knob. Thank fuck I pause before turning it. I have to readjust and wait a moment longer before forcing a polite smile and re-opening the door.

There was a professional response I was prepared to say. There was a moment of clarity that came over me before my gaze set on her once again. But the second I realize she is, in fact, Aubrey Peters the comment vanishes into thin air.

My heart races once again.

"I am so very sorry…" she swallows thickly and my eyes are drawn to her collarbone and then up to her slender neck before she finishes, "that was an accident." She nearly whispers the last bit with a muted laugh lacing her tone. "I do apologize," she repeats as our eyes lock and I struggle to gather my composure.

After clearing my throat, I manage, "Not a worry, Aubrey. I swear I didn't see a thing."

A short huff leaves her and her lips kick up into

even in our *dreams*

an asymmetric simper as she stares back at me. As if judging whether or not I did catch a peek of what was beneath her blouse.

My cock reminds me that I did and I lower the clipboard as I ask, "Did you need any help or?"

"No, no, I've got it," she answers and clears her throat, glancing away as that beautiful blush creeps back up to her cheeks.

I pull out the short stool on wheels and have a seat, "It's nice to see you. We went to-"

"High school. Of course, I remember you," she says so easily, so sweetly and my blood heats remembering how much I coveted her from a distance all those years ago.

"You were good friends with Tommy."

"Right right, you two dated back then."

"Yeah…" she huffs out once again, blowing a strand of hair out of her face. "Now you two are even though. Got to the same base," she jokes and then her smile slips. "Maybe that's a little too soon. A bit awkward," she adds and then clears her throat, the smile slipping and a more serious expression replacing it.

With both hands landing on her knees, she asks, "So my blood work?"

"All normal," I answer and flip the page to double check that I didn't just pull that out of my ass.

All the memories of her across the cafeteria, all the moments our eyes locked and all the tension lays back in my mind as I focus on the checkboxes that run down the clipboard.

"Did you have any concerns?" I question her without looking up, hell bent on doing my job rather than falling trap to nostalgia. She's probably married by now or at least has a boyfriend and she doesn't need her doctor taking advantage of her.

She's quiet a long time and I peek up at her, the paper rustling as I let it fall.

"No, no," she answers quickly and then shrugs. "Just a checkup." She licks her bottom lip before tucking it under, her teeth sinking into it.

My cock reminds me that I'm not just a doctor, but also a red-blooded man who has had a crush on Bree for as long as I can remember.

The clipboard clacks as I set it down on the counter. "Everything looks good, no need to adjust your diet, keep taking those vitamins and all should be just fine," I offer her and then wonder what the hell I just said and praying it sounded professional because all I can focus on is the fact that my erection

even in our *dreams*

is only getting harder with every passing second of her hazel eyes on me.

"When you and Tommy broke up… you said you hated athletes, right?"

"Yeah," she says and then lets her head fall back with a laugh. "Swore them off… even you." I nearly quit lacrosse when I heard she said that. Would have lost my full ride to college.

To say I was head over heels for her is an understatement.

I let a beat pass, my heart pounding as I wonder if I should say it, but glance down at her left hand and think, fuck it, there's no time like the present and she's not wearing a ring. "You've never dated a doctor though, right?"

She laughs a short feminine laugh that brings a warmth over every inch of me. This woman has always had some kind of hold on me. If only she knew it.

"Oh my God," she breaks up the tension. "Sorry, I just… I did get the blood work done for a reason. I've been having really bad allergies for a while and the medicine is making me really drowsy all day and-"

"Gotcha," I straighten my back as I turn towards the clipboard and see what she's prescribed. "We can get you an alternative easy enough." I peer up at her and there's that look again, a longing question in her eyes that I try to ignore. "We can try some things out and see what works," I offer and swallow, my throat suddenly dry.

"Yeah, I've been having some weird dreams with it too."

I could dream of her for days.

"I'll get you a script and leave it at the front desk for you," I offer, letting the clipboard drop to right where it needs to be as I stand. "Anything else, Bree?"

Her lips lift into a gorgeous smile. "You called me Bree," she murmurs.

"Sorry Ms.—"

"Don't you dare," she jokes as she tucks her hair behind her ear. "I just really like hearing you say it… is all."

"Well if it's all the same to you, you can call me Bennet… no need for Doctor."

I second guess the statement the second it's out my mouth. I haven't dated in years and I'm rusty as all hell. With a nervous smile and short nod, silence settles between us and I think I've ruined it.

"Any other concerns before I leave you to it?"

"Just that I'll be single forever," she jokes and then her gaze glances between me and the floor.

Single… If I'm not mistaken, she's hitting on me.

"Are you dating someone?" she dares to ask and that's when all the blood in my head rushes to my dick.

"I'm not …" I answer, swallowing thickly and making doubly sure that the clipboard is in fact still blocking her view so she doesn't know exactly what she does to me and how very little control I have around her.

"Me either.…" she says and adds, "The worst part about being single is going out to restaurants alone."

"Do you want a date?" I ask and then reconsider how I phrased the question. "I mean to a restaurant; we can catch up … if you want?"

"You kind of owe me a drink since you got a free show," she jokes.

I smirk, "Dinner tonight? That seafood place by the lake?"

"A girl is never supposed to accept a date offered the day of." My heart drops but picks right back up when she finishes her thought. "Luckily I'm terrible at dating and I love lobster."

I'm stunned for a moment. I'm going to go out on a date with Bree.

"Not that I would order the lobster," she rushes out the words when I stay silent a little too long.

Fuck, I love how nervous I make her. I hope that's a sign that I get to her too. That would only be fair considering the chokehold she has over me.

"It would be fine if you did," I tell her, offering as charming of a smile as I can manage.

"Yes, tonight sounds wonderful," she agrees and with that I head out, telling her I'll text her and bringing up the clipboard to motion, "this is your number right?"

She nods and then her gaze drops.

Fuck.

"Yes. Yes it is." she says, struggling to bring her eyes back up.

Fuck, fuck, fuck; the clipboard is lowered again as my cheeks blaze and I tell her, "I'll see you tonight then."

Her voice carries behind me as I make my way out as fast as I can, "Looking forward to it."

chapter Three

Aubrey

THE SWING'S GENTLE CREAK IS ALMOST drowned out by the unison laughter from my neighbors. It's become a habit of ours, cocktails and gossip on Marlena's porch right around 4 or 5pm every Wednesday night, depending on how desperate we are for the day to be over. Most of us work from home, we all live on Cedar Lane and Marlena is kind enough to host ... and kind enough to watch us all waddle home if we've had a few too many. I know first-hand Lauren can drag me onto my sofa and will tuck the throw around me if the wine goes down a little too easy.

She's the one next to me on the swing, keeping the rhythm of it with Gemma and Marlena in the wicker chairs across from us. Marlena's patio is a suburban dream design straight from the catalogs. With potted petunias, deep gray painted floors, a viridian door and a white railing, she thought about every detail. Or at least her designer did. Even the straws in her cocktail glasses fit the color palette coming in shades of dark greens and blues.

These three women are the only reason I leave my house some weeks. For laughs and gossip and, glancing down I stir the straw in my drink, a damn good sangria.

"So are they dating then?" Marlena says lowly, a spark of mischief in her eyes and a smile plastered on her face as she questions.

"Well if they aren't," Gemma answers between sips, "they are most certainly screwing."

Lauren claps leaning back in her chair, "It's about time they went for it!"

Gemma's coworkers have been the topic of conversation for weeks now. From the two coworkers staring a little too long, leaving work early at the same time and most recently, staying later together and getting caught red handed.

"I hope they are," my little romantic heart speaks for me, "they would make such a cute couple."

"I'm just happy she's getting laid. It's been years, hasn't it?" Lauren questions. She's far more… reasonable than me. More grounded. Whereas any of these ladies would say I live in a happy little bubble. I guess when you're an editor of fantasy sagas and romance novels it's easy to get lost in a world that lends itself to happily ever afters.

The conversation continues but the typical giddiness is replaced by a nervousness I've felt ever since I left the doctor's office.

Marlena's house is just across the street from me and I find myself glancing up to look at my driveway as Gemma continues filling us in on the details of the office drama.

He should be here in the next twenty minutes.

"What time is he coming again?" Lauren asks and I turn to see all three of them staring at me. Gem is at odds with Marlena in the clothing department, a cotton sundress right beside gray sweats and a simple cotton tee.

With all three set of eyes staring, my ears burn and my face heats. "He said he would pick me up around six."

"I want to know what shoes he's going to wear," Gemma comments as Marlena tells me the pleated navy sundress is perfect. I have a white button down cashmere cardigan to pair with it and white sandals too. Not too dressy but not too casual.

"What shoes?" Lauren scrunches her nose, the ice in her sangria clinking against the glass as she leans forward questioning Gemma's reasoning.

"Well I've noticed if they wear sneakers on the first date they aren't going to put effort in." Marlena laughs and Lauren waves her off, all the while butterflies flutter in my lower belly.

I couldn't count the number of times I thought about Bennet asking me out … while wearing his cleats after a game in high school. Instead of commenting, I simply take another sip of sangria and silently ask the cocktail to calm my nerves.

It doesn't seem to be helping. With every minute that passes, the anxiousness only soars.

"It's going to be fine," Lauren reassures me as the porch swing ebbs and flows. Her brow is arched as she brings the straw to her lips. She eyes me like she knows I'm overthinking everything. I've known these women for all my life in this small town, so they probably know every thought flying through my head right now.

"At least you know he likes your boobs," Marlena says with a shrug and girlish smile and Gemma snickers into her drink before covering her grin.

Lauren doesn't try to hide her laugh.

"I'm not even sure he really saw," I tell them as I yet again glance up to check my driveway.

They all answer in unison, "He saw."

"There is a zero chance he didn't see." Lauren puts a finality on it.

A violent blush creeps into my cheeks. I almost tell them what I saw as he left the room, but I keep that piece of information to myself. At least for now, another sangria and depending on how tonight goes and I might spill it.

There's a golden rule with these wine down Wednesdays: what's confessed on Marlena's porch, stays on Marlena's porch.

chapter Four

Bennet

YOU LEARN SOMETHING NEW EVERY DAY. As I read the message from Steve, a good buddy of mine and currently my landlord since I'm renting his place until I find my own, my brow cocks.

Tommy moved away and has four kids.

He adds: *So go for it. We all thought you two were going to get together after high school anyway.*

I almost text him, Maybe we would have, if I hadn't

moved away. I delete the message and let out an uneasy sigh. It's a simple story. I had a crush on Bree, but I was too young and dumb and nervous with puppy dog feelings to do anything about it. Then I left for college, then med school, then an internship and I've only just come back.

I'm damn surprised, and damn lucky too, that she's single. Even more surprised that the first week back we stumbled into each other's paths like we did.

My phone pings in my hand as I sit in my parked car at the end of her drive alerting me to another text from Steve: *That's my two cents anyway. He's gone, she's single, go for it.*

This is a small town and no one ever really leaves, so it's surprising Tommy settled down up north. Maybe I should send him a thank you card, I think as I glance between my phone and Bree's front door.

I think I just might, I text Tommy as if I'm not parked in her driveway as we speak.

The corner of my lip picks up into an asymmetric grin, knowing there shouldn't be any issues. Steve would have given me the heads up if there was anything to worry about. In a small town, there's always someone spreading gossip or starting up shit. There's always someone who has feelings for someone else or toes being stepped on as a new lover comes in.

The unnecessary bullshit is why I left this place but I missed my family, my friends… and it's home. This small town will always be home for me.

"Bennet," a feminine voice calls out and I glance across the paved street to a raised ranch on Cedar Lane. The porch swing rocks as someone raises a glass to me and across her two other women wave. All the while, my eyes are drawn to a beautiful woman in an easy sundress and heels, covering her face as if she's embarrassed by her friends.

My smile widens, Bree. Just as I open the door, my phone pings again and it's Steve: *You always had a crush on her, didn't you?*

We all knew on the team

Well no one told me, I quickly type out and before I can add that I'm with her now, he texts: *Pretty sure you knew you had a crush on her.*

Bree's heels drown out the chuckle that leaves me and I slip my phone in my pocket just in time to look up and see her only a foot away.

"Just let me run in and grab my purse," she motions towards the door as an easy breeze blows by and my heart skips a beat. I give her a short nod and take in every inch of her.

There's something that stirs inside of me, telling me this was meant to be. A little deja vu, like in some other life, it wouldn't be our first date, this would have been a normal day for us. I get home from work, she slips off her friend's porch to greet me with a kiss.

No kiss for me though, instead I get a gorgeous view of her beautiful backside as she turns to head towards the door.

"She looks breathtaking doesn't she?" Lauren calls out from the porch. I'm not sure if it's her house or one of the two other women, Marlena and ... someone I don't quite recognize from a distance but I bet if I heard her voice, I'd know who it is.

We all grew up together and names and stories have flooded me this week since I've been back.

"She does," I rock on my heels, raising my voice so Lauren can hear me and just as I slip my hands into my pocket, I hear a small squeal and a thud and turn to see Bree, face down on the sidewalk.

The peanut gallery lets out a collective groan and one of them comments just loud enough that I can hear, "Shit, that had to hurt."

ever in our *dreams*

With quick strides I head to Aubrey, who's grimacing but trying to play it off.

"What happened?"

"I just..." she starts and then winces and grabs her ankle.

"You fell?" I question and check the ground for what she tripped over.

"It's fine," she waves me off but when I hold my hand out to her, she places hers in mine and allows me to help her up. She's dainty in my hands and I find myself bracing her for longer than probably needed. Her soft curve fits perfectly.

Her hazel eyes peer up at me and there's a spark that's reignited. Her breath hitches and she swallows thickly before pointing to the house.

"I just have to," she starts but isn't able to finish as our gaze locks.

"Grab your purse, right," I finish for her and loosen up my grip.

She takes a single step, not breaking eye contact but then the tension is cut.

"Oh," she winces, taking in a sharp breath.

"I might need to walk this off actually," she comments and scrunches her face.

"Let me just check it, you could have sprained

your ankle." Before she can object, I wrap my arm around her waist and help her up the steps.

She's putting weight on it, and I imagine she's just fine, but having a quick look to make sure everything's alright won't hurt.

"Thanks," she whispers and when I peek down at her, that spark hits again and this time it slips past my racing heart, down lower, to the one part of me that I wish wouldn't interject right now. I clear my throat and think of every possible thing I can to soften my growing erection.

What am I? A freaking school boy going through puberty?

With heat rising up my neck, I've never been more embarrassed but luckily, Bree doesn't seem to notice.

"I would do this. They all told me not to mess it up and look at me now," she jokes as she pushes the door open with a soft creak. I laugh along with her, taking in her foyer. It's modern but quaint. The houses on Cedar Lane have been here for years and I can tell she's put work into her home. The wall going up the stairs is a dark green, almost emerald with white and copper accents of picture frames and paintings.

To the left, it's a soft cream and leads straight into her kitchen.

She leaves me as I stand in the foyer, taking one step and then another. "See I'm fine."

"Just have a seat and let me have a look at you," I tell her and then my cock reminds me of every fantasy I've ever had of being this close to Aubrey Peters.

She leads me through the kitchen, which is tidied up with a fresh bouquet of wildflowers in a vase in the middle of the island, to the cozy living room. It's painted a soft gray, but there are pops of color everywhere you look. From the pale blue crochet throw blanket on the back of the deep navy velvet sofa to the abstract painting hung on the wall behind it that contains nearly every color in varying smudges.

All of the feminine touches feel like her.

"It's a little much, I know," she jokes as she lowers herself to the sofa.

"Not judging," I hold up both hands and then lower myself to my knees in front of her. I'm careful as I take her ankle in my hand.

"I'm fine. I already feel just fine," she reassures me and my knowledge agrees with her. No bruising, no swelling. "I'm just a little clumsy when my crush is staring at my behind," she comments and when I glance up to ask how she knows where I was looking, she has her phone in her hand.

She smirks at me, the sexiest most tempting smirk I've ever seen on a woman. "Lauren text me and it caught me off guard."

"Ah," I nod, letting her foot drop easily, "so it's my fault?"

"I'm not saying that," she laughs but then bites down on her lower lip, "but a kiss might make it up to me."

My heart hammers in my chest. "You don't waste time, do you?" I wonder if she's feeling the same tension I am.

"I suppose it depends on how you look at it, I've had a crush on you since high school," she almost whispers the confession and leans forward just slightly. Unfortunately, it's just as I was getting up and to avoid her falling into me, her hands come out, landing on my chest.

Her hands on mine, and this position, I can't help but wrap my arm around her waist and pull her off the sofa, landing a small kiss on her lips.

I anticipate her standing, but she lowers herself to the floor beneath me, deepening the kiss, teasing me, tempting me, and I have never wanted for more in my life.

Aubrey

My chest rises and falls as my breathing quickens. I swear I must be blushing from head to toe with how hot my entire body is all of a sudden. He doesn't move and I don't dare move either. My gaze shifts lower though, back to his lips before bringing them to his baby blue gaze. The spark is undeniable and at this moment every single dating rule doesn't mean a damn thing.

The one specifically about waiting for three dates before sex. With his masculine scent filling my lungs and his large frame surrounding me as I lay under him, all I can think about is how badly I want him to take me right here. It's almost like a dream come true, one I've had a hundred times before.

It's that memory of the dreams I've had time and time again that makes me bite my lip. I know I shouldn't do it, every rule book would tell me not to. But I'm too damn scared that I'll never get this chance again.

With my heart pounding, I lift my lips to his, propping myself up this time to reach him. At first his lips are firm, his gaze hesitant, but when I kiss him again, his lips mold to mine and I part his seam with the tip of my tongue.

The heat is instant and I moan into his mouth, desperate for more. Desperate for all of him right now.

My fingers spear through his hair. My nails scrape gently against his scalp as he deepens the kiss, letting a low groan vibrate up his chest. I can't help the smile that begs to appear.

His breathing is heavy, his hands braced on either side of me as he towers over me on the floor.

"I've wanted you for so long," I whisper against his lips when the kiss finally breaks.

His brow raises just slightly as I catch my lip between my teeth and ever so slowly, let the tips of my fingers find the top button of his collared shirt.

His expression softens as his gaze falls down my body, taking me in, inch by inch and an insecurity I haven't felt in years resurfaces.

My heart races as I carefully undo the button and

wait for his eyes to find mine again and when they do, a question lingers there. A hesitation that brings fear.

"Are you sure… you want to?" he questions in a low murmur.

A moment passes, one that feels far too long although it's only a single tick of the clock.

"Yes," I breathe and in an instant, he's on me. His lips on mine and then down my neck, possessively taking me with a rapture I know too well. With my neck arched, I offer him more, but he stops short above my breasts to pull his shirt over his head in a single swift movement.

Taught tanned skin, rippling muscle and powerful shoulders trap me in as he drops the shirt carelessly to the floor.

I'm speechless at the sight of him. As if he's a sex God wrapped up in a suit and stripped down just for me.

My reaction must be plastered on my face, because as he unbuckles his belt and then kicks off his pants, he smirks.

I swallow thickly, as the buckle clanks on the floor. His bulge is even larger than I thought it was in the office. I almost convinced myself I was giving him more credit than deserved. As if my imagination made it appear larger than it was.

Nope. He is in fact ... intimidating.

"Your turn, Bree baby," he murmurs in a deep timbre and my eyes reach his heated gaze.

Thump. My heart beats faster as I tug my dress down. Lust plays between us as he helps me strip. As my bra falls, he stares at my breasts with a look in his eyes of utter temptation before dipping down to suck a nipple into his mouth. His teeth graze my sensitized skin, nipping as he toys with me. It's as if he has a direct link to my clit with the singular act.

My head falls back and before I know it, I'm beneath him, bared to him and the head of his cock presses gently against me.

He kisses me once, before pulling back, his eyes piercing into mine as he pushes himself steadily and deeply into me. The slight pain of being stretched is far outmatched by the pleasure of being filled by him. He stays there, buried deep inside of me as my head thrashes from one side to the other as I adjust for him. He kisses my neck with a tenderness as he pulls out slowly, before thrusting in with a skill that pulls a moan of pleasure from me that I did not consciously give.

even in our *dreams*

"I always told myself if ever I had a chance with you, I would go slow," he whispers at the shell of my ear as he withdraws slowly once again but then quickly thrusts, forcing me to hold onto him, my nails digging into his back. Pleasure wraps around me all at once, making my head dizzy and my breathing ragged. He finishes the thought, "I can't though, not when you feel this fucking good." And with that, he ruts into me, pistoning his hips and a cold sweat breaks out along my skin as pleasure takes over.

He groans once as he thrusts harder, the sexiest sound. He grips my hips, keeping me where he wants me and as he intensifies his pace, he fucks me like he already knows every inch of me and exactly how to bring me to the highest high.

As I come undone, pulsing around his thick length, he groans in the crook of my neck, "Fuck, Bree," and thrusts himself one more time before finding his release.

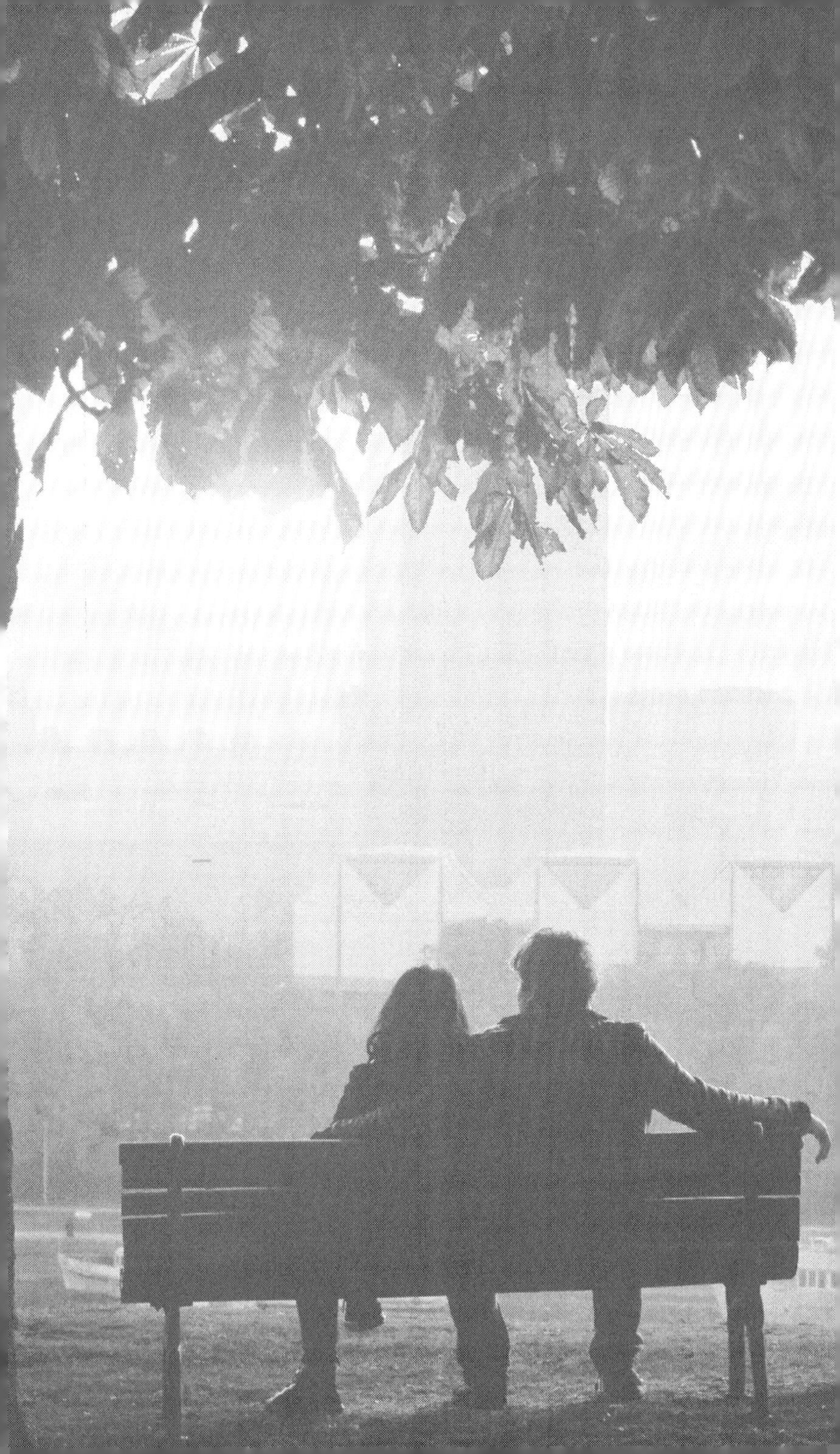

chapter

Five

Aubrey

"I'M SORRY, I'M GOING TO NEED YOU TO tell me that one more time..." Lauren starts, "You didn't get the wining and dining, you just got the sixty-nining?" With a raised brow my closest friend for over a decade smirks at me from where she's perched on the porch swing.

With their glasses of prosecco and sangria respectively Marlena and Gemma eye me from their seats across from us. Both of them are still giddy from the tidbit I let slip. In black leggings and a sleeveless button down with a black and white floral print, I let the swing rock once and pause. The wind blows by and I swear not a soul on Marlena's porch dares to breathe.

"First of all, no judging," I start, leaning back in the swing and pulling my legs up so the heels of my feet rest on the edge of the swing. Lauren is the only one in PJs, she's been in them all day. The flannel pants are at odds with the work attire the other two wear as they let out squeals of joy.

"Not judging, I'm impressed-" Lauren states with a grin. Her wide eyes don't leave me and the heat rolls up from my chest to my temples.

"What's the second of all?" Marlena questions behind her glass. I bet her cheeks hurt; she's grinning so wide.

It's been a while, a very long while, since I've been with someone intimately. And last night… well I can still feel him. The sweet ache reminded me of last night every time I sat down or adjusted in my seat.

"We're going out tonight. In fifteen minutes."

"Seafood?" Gem questions.

"A drive in actually." The swing creaks as it rocks.

"To see a movie?"

"Yeah. It should be fun."

even in our *dreams*

"I bet you guys are going to do it in the back of Steve's truck," Marlena comments around a snicker.

"Oh my God Marlena!" Lauren scolds comically.

Gemma only laughs and then asks how many sangrias she's had and if Lauren put extra liquor in tonight.

My cheeks heat and I wave her off. "It's Steve's truck so that'll be a big no."

"You two got it on the first night… like damn."

"I mean it's a decade or more of sexual tension. Flood gates had to come down sooner rather than later," Lauren shrugs.

I'm going to have to agree with that. "I honestly don't know what came over me."

Little moments from last night flick through my mind. From the way he made me come undone, to the moments after when he kissed my shoulder and held me.

"How did he get out of taking you to dinner?"

"What do you mean? It was—"

"Like I get it, you're hurt, the doctor's hands are all over you. It's totally the minimal plot to a porno, but—"

"Oh my God, take her sangria away," Lauren jokes as Marlena barks out a laugh.

"It was my idea actually…," that heat comes back with full force, "because as we were kissing after… like… you know round two," I barely get out the last part, downing my drink as my friends all lean back in their seats, Marlena clapping and Gemma staring at me wide eyed.

"Twice?" Lauren questions, also leaning back on her half of the swing to stare me down.

I can't help the laughter that comes over me. I shake my head and hand over my mouth, "Twice before dinner was delivered… and once after."

As my friends react to the news of my very productive night, Lauren hushes them at the sound of a car parking. "He's here," Lauren whispers and it only makes Marlena laugh harder.

"Get her," Lauren jokes to Gemma who can't help but to laugh too.

It only takes a moment for them to pull it together and in that time, Bennet crosses the street and waits for me by Marlena's picket fence.

"Hello ladies," Bennet greets us. I'm struck for a moment, taking him in as he looks over his shoulder back at Steve's truck he borrowed just for tonight. Blue jeans look damn good on him and the white tee is stretched across his broad shoulders. He's always wanted to be a doctor, but he wears blue collar well.

When his pale blue eyes reach mine, his lip turns up and a warmth flows through me.

"How are you doing Bennet?" Lauren asks.

"You came to steal her away from us?" Gemma calls out after.

He lets out a rough chuckle and I swear that deep masculine sound does something to me. There's not just a spark of chemistry as I climb out of the seat and slip on my simple sandals, and grab my black clutch and white jean jacket, it's as if my entire body is on fire, magnetized and pulled to him.

"You can slow down. You don't have to run." Lauren murmurs the joke so only I can hear as Bennet answers Gemma, "If it's alright with you three, that's my plan."

I'm already off the porch when they joke with him that he can have me for tonight but I better be home by ten.

He opens the gate for me and as we wave goodbye, his arm wraps around my waist. It's all too natural, all too comfortable. All too fast. And yet, I love it.

As he opens the truck door for me, it creaks. Steve's truck is old and high off the ground for me.

It's perfect for the drive in though. I peek in the back of the blue truck that's pale from age and there's a basket and blankets, pillows too. I have to bite down on my lip to keep my smile from growing.

"Do I need to help you up?" he asks in a rough timbre that sends a sweet shiver of want down my shoulders. I'm trapped there, between the truck and his tall frame. His scent wraps around me as the wind blows and I get up on my tiptoes, giving him a peck on the lips before climbing in.

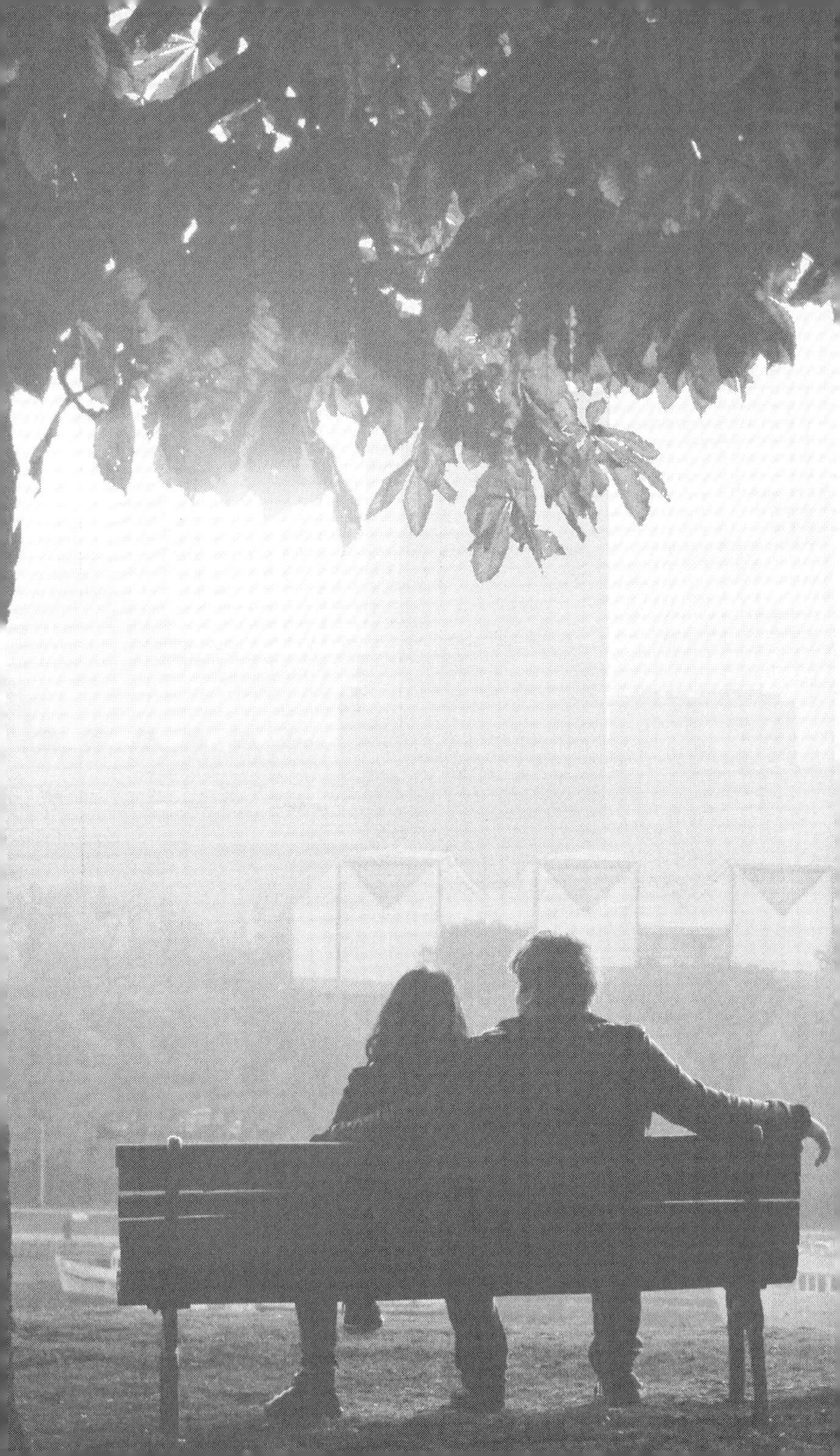

chapter

Six

Bennet

The dim light from the projected screen casts down on her shoulders.

It's a picture-perfect setting, apart from the awful movie.

It's some comedy action and I lost the plot as soon as she cuddled up next to me, her hand resting on my leg… very close to a body part of mine that doesn't need to be a part of tonight. All I can think about as we lay back in the flatbed of my friend's truck, under a white cotton comforter, is how easy this is.

How comfortable it all feels. How she fits perfectly next to me, the pillows behind us, half a dozen of them, a box of sour candy and a bucket of popcorn in my lap.

"Is it alright if I move the bucket?" Bree asks and it takes me a moment before I catch on to her making light of what happened in the office.

Just as my expression shows the realization, she lets out the sweetest laugh.

"I'm sorry, I didn't mean to tease," she says with her shoulders shaking gently.

"I don't think for a single second that you didn't mean to tease."

"Okay maybe I did. Maybe I also wanted to move the popcorn so I could do this…" she starts and then I watch as she moves the bucket, placing it on the other side of her and then kisses me. A hand on my cheek, her soft palm against my five o'clock shadow. It's soft and sweet. It's just like her.

She nuzzles down next to me, leaving a warmth to spread through me.

Something flashes across the screen and catches her attention before I can make a single comment.

even in our *dreams*

Aubrey is … unexpected. I keep thinking I need to be careful with her. That I can't fuck this up. Yet here she is, just having fun.

And there it is. She's just having fun.

The realization dawns on me as she watches the scene play out ahead of us. It's an anxiousness that comes over me as I glance down at her wondering if this is just a good time for her, or if she's interested in more.

"Movie is awful," she murmurs, and then glances up at me.

"I'm so glad you said so," I comment back and stretch my arm above my head before laying it on the pillow so I can rest my head on my hand.

"So what did you do after high school?"

She smirks at me, "Small talk?"

"Or we could watch the movie," I offer with a grin.

She gets comfortable beside me, telling me about how she's an editor for a publishing house.

The conversation carries on easily as she updates me on how it happened and the stories she's been a part of. "A couple were turned into TV shows."

"No kidding," I comment without thinking, letting my brow raise with surprise.

"That's right." Pride shines in her eyes but there's still a shyness and vulnerability about her.

"Look at you, fancy editor."

"I mean I'm not a fancy *doctor*."

"Me neither, just a regular doctor."

She chuckles at my cheesy joke and I wish I could shake off the nerves. I'd like to tell her how lonely it was. Studying and working, interning and all the sleepless nights. I missed this town, I missed out on so much.

"I'm just happy to be back home and that the family practice had an opening."

She smiles shyly, seeming to debate on what she wants to say next but she settles with, "I'm happy you're back too."

God damn, she's so beautiful, smart and funny. I just don't get it. "How are you single?"

"You know you're not supposed to ask that question," she comments with a somewhat serious tone.

My throat tightens slightly, thinking I might be messing this up but also… that there might be something I don't know.

"I just never clicked with anyone I guess," she comments off handily.

even in our dreams

A beat passes and I gather up the nerve to just fucking ask her.

"So … the two of us…" I prepare to ask the obvious question. *Is it serious? Or just messing around?* I haven't told a soul what happened the other night. If we're on different pages, which could very well be the case, the town would catch wind of it fast and I don't need to come back home to be the center of gossip.

"What about us?" she asks.

"I'm just wondering…" I start and then readjust, moving the pillow behind me as I clear my throat to get comfortable. As I do, I wrap an arm around Bree. She fits there perfectly, taking the opportunity to scoot closer.

"I like the two of us," she answers with a sensual whisper, turning onto her side and brushing the tip of her nose along my chin. I'm rock hard instantly.

This drive in theater has been here for as long as I can remember. More than a time or two my friends and I would drive out, some would have girlfriends and I pictured Bree here too. A decade has passed and that dream has finally come to life.

At that thought, she kisses me. It's a quick peck but her hand rests on my chest, her hair sweeps along my shoulder. It's more than just a kiss. She whispers, biting down on a smile as she pulls back and then looks me in the eye, "I really really like us."

With her doe eyes and that blush hitting her cheeks.

"I really really like us too," I tell her, dropping my voice down as I stare at her lips. Her teeth sink into her bottom one before she leans in, kissing me again. This time I'm prepared and my hand rests on the small of her back, my other reaches up behind her, bracing her back with my hand at the back of her neck. Her lips mold to mine and when I brush the tip of my tongue along her seam, she parts for me.

The feminine moan that slips from her as I deepen the kiss is fucking heaven.

My tongue strokes along hers and precum leaks from my cock.

Fuck. She can't think I just want sex from her. But even as the thought hits me, she makes a move to straddle me, never taking her lips from mine.

"People might see," I protest with weakest fucking protest between open mouthed kisses down her neck. She gives me another of those sweet gasps and I rake my teeth along her neck.

"I can be quiet," she murmurs as her breasts press against my chest.

With that promise, my hands roam down her body. I cup her ass as she pulls the blanket up around us.

There are only ten vehicles parked up here on the hill. We probably know every single driver. There's not a chance in hell we're going all the way up here. They'll see and I'll be damned if I let anyone else hear these addictive moans she's giving me.

Possessiveness grips a hold of me as I move her under me. She gasps, at first, shocked from the move, and her nails dig into my shoulders as she holds on. Then she lets out a feminine laugh and kisses me again, one of those short pecks. With her beneath me, I pepper kisses down her neck before coming back up. All the while she writhes under me.

I whisper at the shell of her ear, "You have no idea how much I want to taste you right now."

Goosebumps flow down her shoulder as she shivers beneath me with lust filled eyes.

"You want to stay the night at my place," she questions, and as she does, she presses herself against me. Her eyes widen slightly as she realizes there's more that I want to do than just eat her out.

She must read the thought racing through my mind: that would make the town talk.

"You could sneak out in the morning?" she offers like it's a question.

"You must really want me to stay over." I rock myself into her

"Maybe I just want to get in bed with you," she comments and settles down into the pillows beneath me.

Is that all you want me for? I almost ask her. Before I can, she reaches up, wrapping her hands behind my head and pulls me down to her with another kiss.

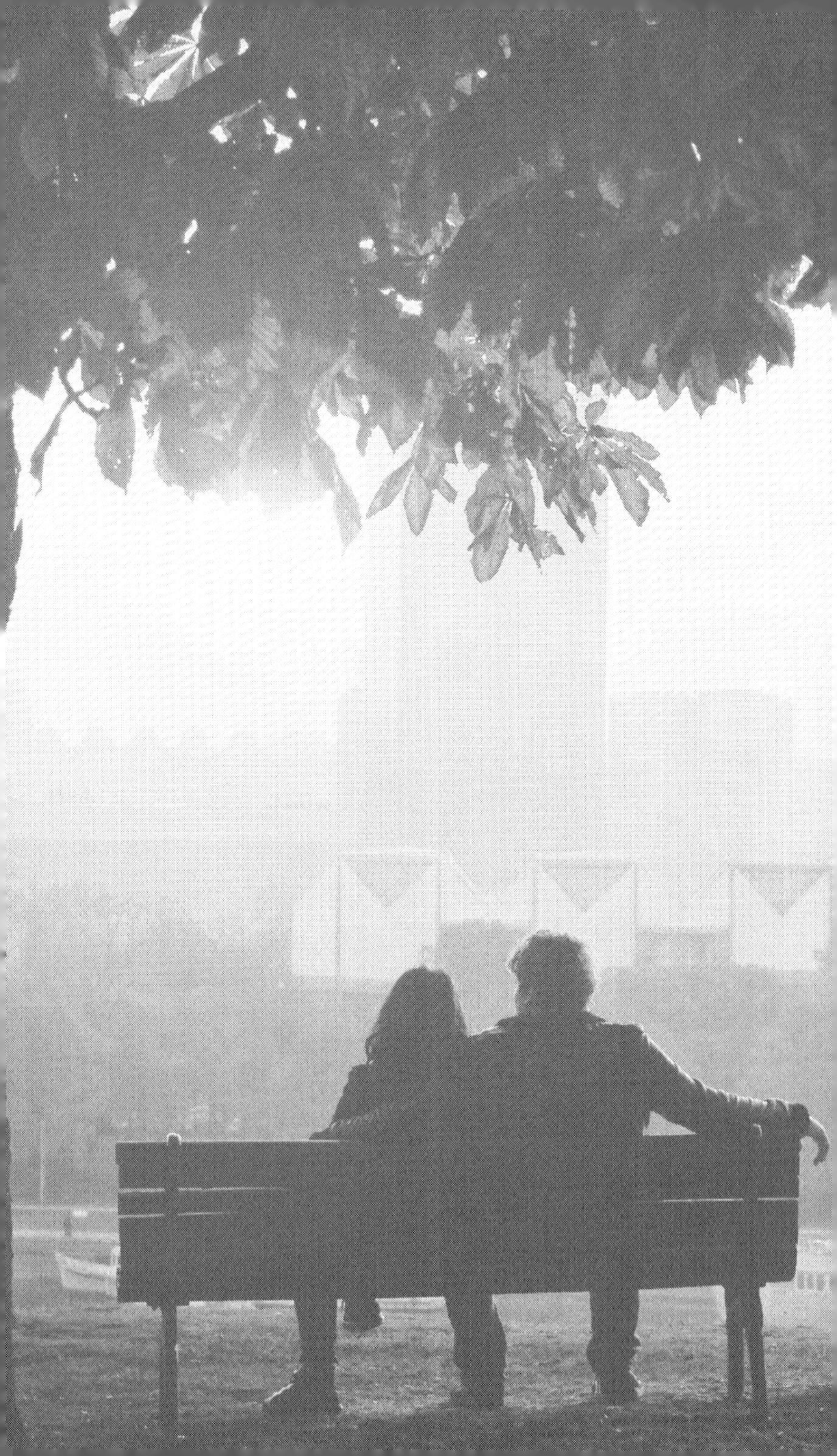

chapter Seven

Aubrey

"You're cooking?" Lauren's tone is skeptical as she and Gemma slip into the kitchen, Marlena must be the one closing the door as I peek over my shoulder.

"I am," I answer as I stir the pot. The garlic bread is in the toaster, and store bought, same as the pasta.

"You're cooking Bennet dinner tonight," Lauren asks to clarify and then shares a glance with Gemma as Marlena enters the kitchen. She's the first to pull out a stool and reach for the red wine at the table while Gemma and Lauren stare back at me expectantly. "What? He had a long week and he's going to a conference next week-"

"You're only supposed to cook for a man if you want him to move in," Gemma comments with a smirk. Lauren's smile widens along with Gemma all the while Marlena fills her glass and couldn't care less about the two of them teasing me.

"Is that true?" I question with a smirk as I tap the wooden spoon on the edge of the saucepan. The red sauce is my grandmother's recipe and the scent of the garlic and herbs makes my mouth water. I'm not the best cook in the world, but this sauce is going to seal the deal.

"Yeah. You only cook for a man in your own house if you want him to move in." As Gemma lays out the statement as if it's fact she finally pulls out the stool. "In his house if you want to move in with him… There's a book about it or a blog or something. I read it somewhere."

Lauren laughs as she pulls out her stool. "Yeah okay," I comment and then I turn around to face the trio all lined up at the granite countertop… "Well what if I do want him to move in?"

It's been three weeks of seeing him, occasional sleep overs and sneaking out, tip toeing about how perfect we are. Neither of us has put a label on it, but we talk every day and we can't keep our hands off of each other.

"Are you out of your mind?" Lauren objects immediately and just before I was going to add that it seems logical. I bite back that thought and give a different response.

"I don't think so," I shrug. One breath in as three sets of shocked eyes stare back at me. "I think I might love him."

"You are out of your ever-loving mind," Gemma states again as if it's fact.

"You can't be in love with someone you've only been dating for a week."

"Three weeks... if you round up," I rebut.

"Lauren tell her," Gemma elbows Lauren and Marlena simply clings to her glass.

As Lauren shakes her head she comically empties the bottle into her glass and then looks at me with the empty bottle in hand and her brow raised.

"What? I have another bottle." Marlena breaks her silence to laugh at my joke.

"He could be using you for sex," Gem offers.

"Well hold on now-" I start to defend him but Marlena speaks up. "Is he telling people you're dating?"

"I don't think so, but mostly because I asked him not to ... you know how this town likes to talk and I didn't want anyone knowing he was sleeping over."

Lauren pipes up with a "strike one," at the same time Marlena asks, "And are you telling people you're dating?"

I turn my back to stir the pot but first point the wooden spoon at them, "You are my only friends so that would be a yes."

A quick stir and a check on the pasta proves that dinner is almost done and I'm going to need to kick the three of them out. I know they only came over for a quick update and now they have it so they can take the glasses of wine as party favors.

It's quiet when I turn back around to face them. "Do I need to make it social media official?"

"I think you're in lust." Gemma comments and I take the four steps to the counter, grabbing the edges of it with both of my hands as I lean over to set my friends straight.

They might be protective and I might be rushing things but I'm not getting any younger and I know exactly what I want.

even in our *dreams*

"Can't I be in lust and in love?"

"Did you just say love?" Lauren questions but not in her motherly tone, there's a smile that graces her lips. Gemma's glass of wine stops at her lips and she waits for the answer too.

"Do I want to fuck him?" I ask them rhetorically and as I say, "yes I do," Marlena attempts to hush me and Lauren waves her hand at me to stop. "No, I need to get this off my chest." I busy my hands with the apron knot and get out all of the thoughts that have been keeping me up the nights he's not with me.

"Do I enjoy being around him, I do."

"Bree-" Lauren tries to backtrack but I don't let her.

"Do I want to maybe make babies with him? Yeah. He'd make adorable freaking babies and he has the patience of a saint to deal with me." When I look up, tossing the apron on the counter, Lauren covers her face which is bright red. Gemma mouths, "Shut up," and Marlena's focus is directly behind me. "Hey Bennet," she says in a voice that has Lauren and Gemma cracking up.

"I have been told I am a patient man," his masculine voice says behind me and I swear I couldn't shut my mouth if I had both hands on my chin. The amount of embarrassment is unreal.

"We were just going…" Lauren snags her glass and motions for the girls to follow her before mouthing, "Don't kill me," on her way out.

"How long have you been standing there?"

"Since your friends tried to get you to 'hush it' I think was the exact phrase."

"Welp, you have to taste that sauce Bennet," Marlena says, forcing a smile back as she pulls the stool out and then rushes after Lauren and Gemma, both of whom owe me a therapy session.

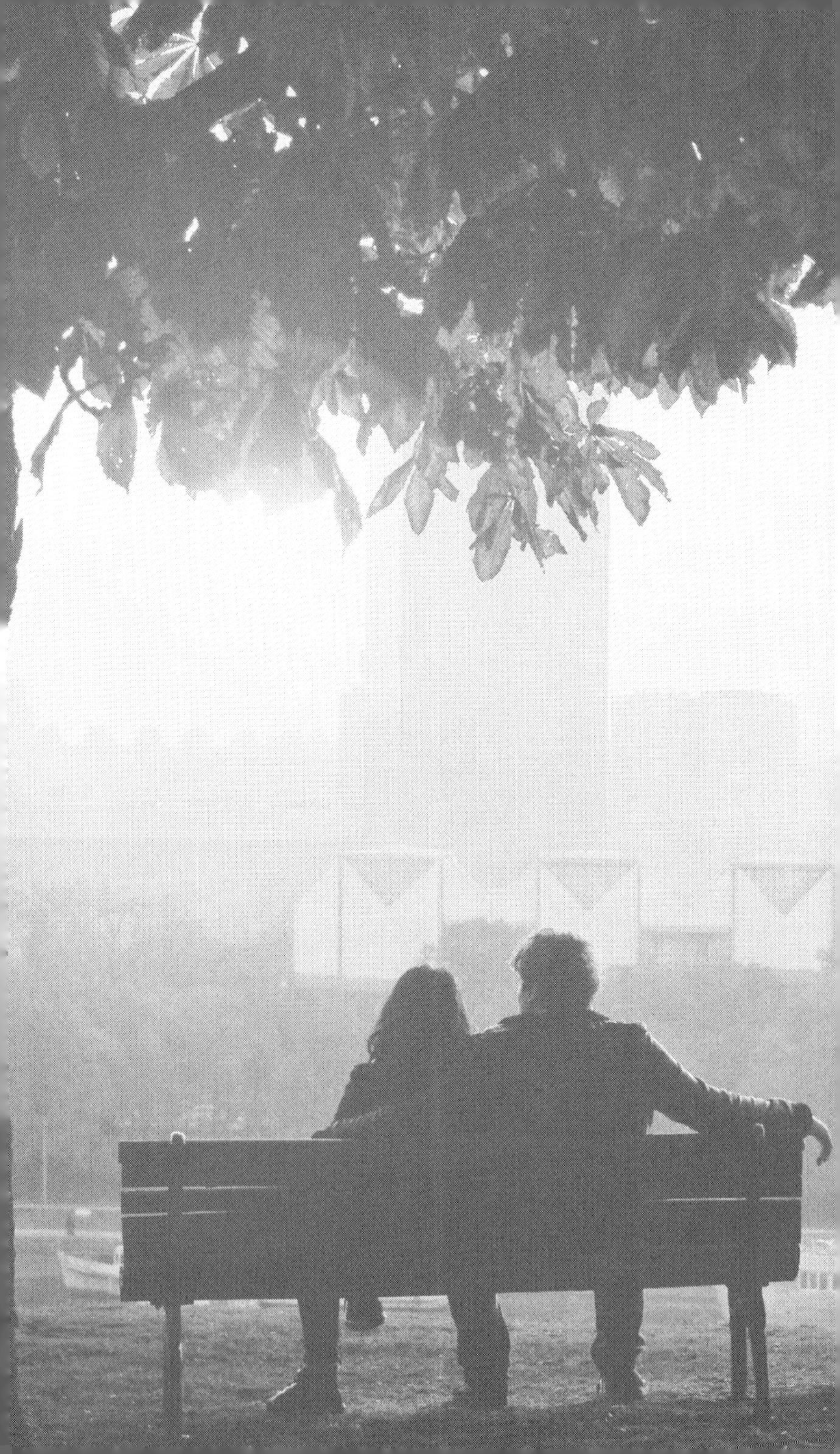

chapter Eight

Bennet

WITH AN ELBOW ON THE COUNTER and a fist over my smile, I can't help the way I feel about Bree. She's adorable when she's nervous.

Ever since her friends left, she busied herself with plating dinner.

"Really I can help," I offer again from where I'm seated on the stool her friend Lauren was in just a moment ago.

"Nope, no, no you just stay put," she tells me with her back to me and as she shakes her head, her body moves with the movement, and the apron wrapped around her waist shows off her curves. In just black leggings and a loose fitting blouse, her outfit should appear casual, but it doesn't at all, much like tonight.

I know damn well her cooking dinner is more than just giving me a night off from a long work week.

"It smells delicious," I tell her and she finally looks back at me with those doe eyes. Her tempting lips pull into a small smile. "It's my grandmother's recipe."

"Really?"

"Well the sauce is. Not … anything else."

As she grabs a bottle of wine to open, I scoot the stool back and insist, "Let me."

I watch her as I open the bottle. The cork pops and I find myself pouring both of us a decent size glass.

"I would try to make her Chicken cacciatore one-pot with orzo," she tells me as she mixes the sauce into the pasta and plates it, her curves tempting me with the movement. "I was editing this cookbook once and I asked the author about it because I wanted so badly to recreate that dish. Long story short, it did not go well. I am not a chef and I know my limits, but I can

even in our *dreams*

at least make the sauce she taught me to make." With that she licks a small bit of sauce from the tip of her finger and lets out the softest, "mmmm."

I have to close my eyes and will my dick to stop twitching. I swear everything this woman does makes me hard.

With a half twirl, she turns with a plate in each hand and places them on the island counter. "Dinner is served," she states with a smile and then perks up, "oh, or do you want to eat at the dining room table?"

"Here's fine," I answer and hand her the glass of cabernet which she accepts with both hands.

"Thank you," she says and takes a sip while I find my seat next to hers.

"I've never thought of myself as the domestic type, but you have me thinking I'm a changed man," I joke with her and motion to the counter.

"Domestic ... that's a word for it." She focuses on the plate in front of her, twirling her spoon between stolen glances.

I take a bite and damn, she wasn't joking. A short groan of satisfaction leaves me.

"It's good right?" She smiles and then takes a bite herself.

"Damn good."

Lifting her glass she says, "Cheers to a relaxing night, with good food and good company." With a smirk on my lips, I clink my glass against hers.

"I'll cheers to that."

We share a look and a blush rises to her cheeks instantly before she tears her eyes away and turns her attention to the pasta. I don't stop staring at her though. We should talk about what I overheard.

"Well I do need to find a place soon," I start. "Renting from Steve was a temporary decision."

She tilts her head, reaches for her wine, and then glances from narrowed eyes. "How much exactly did you hear earlier?"

"Enough," I admit and then gather up sauce in the thick buttered and toasted garlic bread. "In my defense, I didn't tip toe or anything. And you did tell me to 'just come on in.'"

With a gulp, the sound of her swallowing is comical. "Alright then."

I let out a huff of a laugh and then ease her nerves. "I don't know if we should move in, but I could extend the lease with Steve and maybe spend more time here?"

Hesitant eyes look back at me. "I was mostly just joking." Her expression is the most vulnerable I've

even in our *dreams*

ever seen. Like she thinks I might bail. That's not going to fucking happen.

"You want to come down to Austin after the conference? We could stay a little while in a hotel together?"

"I'd have to work but I could work anywhere—you know if you want company

"I would like *your* company… I more than like your company, Bree."

Her throat tightens as she audibly swallows again. For a woman who knows what she wants, she's awfully quiet.

"Listen Bree—I might not be ready for kids just yet. But I am ready to say I want this with you," I motion between us, "more of this, more of us. I have feelings for you."

She smiles shyly, glancing between her fork on her plate and me. "Feelings you say?" Although she's teasing me, there's not a word I've said that I don't mean.

"I've worked myself to death for years and the only thing that's snapped me out of it is you, Bree. We can do this at whatever pace you need. I would like to at least tell this damn town I'm seeing you before I move in and before we talk about all that."

She's quiet as those beautiful hazel eyes stare back

at me. My heart races and I almost wonder if I said the wrong thing. "You think you'd like that?"

"I think ... I'm dreaming," she tells me.

The smirk comes easy and relief floods through me. "That's funny, cause I was thinking that too when I heard you going off about how you feel about me." I almost say, 'I think I might be in love with you, Bree.' Almost, but I bite it back.

She bites down on her lip, still quiet but content.

"Let's just keep doing what we're doing?"

"For dessert can we have sex?"

A rough chuckle leaves me, "Dammit Bree, I'm trying to be good for you."

"You have no idea how good for me you are Bennet." When she looks at me like that, with that look in her eyes and that smile, a peace comes over me. A feeling of home and like everything is the way it's supposed to be.

I'm not sure what the dating rules are, but I know that's the night I dropped all pretense and I fell in love with Aubrey. Head over heels in love with her.

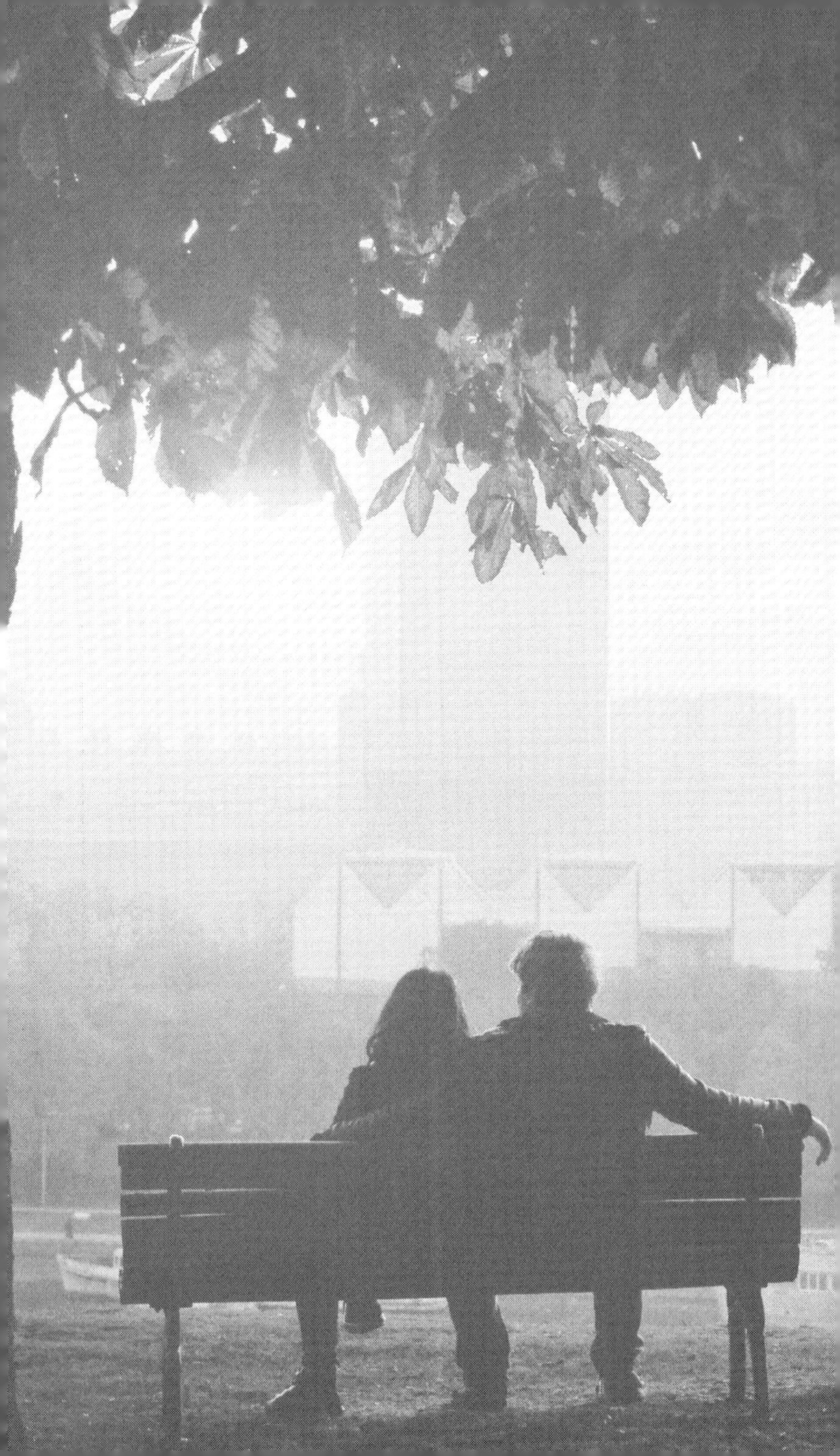

Epilogue

Aubrey

MY VISION IS ONLY BLURRY FOR A MOMENT before I rub my eyes, take in a steadying breath and sip the room temperature coffee without tasting a thing. The moment I see our picture on the counter from across the kitchen where I'm perched, the tears threaten again.

Before it can overwhelm me like it's done this past month, my phone rings and I couldn't be more grateful. I hate being alone through all of this.

Especially at night. My only moment of reprieve is in my dreams.

"Hello," I manage while swiping under my eyes with the back of my hand. Tilting the phone, I take in a calming breath that Gemma won't be able to hear.

"Good morning love," she starts and I'd say good morning back if I could. Instead my bottom lip wobbles.

"Just checking on you," she adds in the absence of a response from me.

"Morning," I breathe out and then stare down at my cup. I want to say thank you. I want to ask her to come over. I want for so much but it's all too numbing to say out loud.

I wish none of this was real.

"Did you schedule that doc appt?"

"Yeah," I answer and then press the sleeve of my cream sweater to my face. "Just trying to get myself together."

"The mornings and nights are hard," she tells me as if she knows. As if any of my friends know. "It's going to be okay," she adds.

The truth rushes out of me, "I just wish I knew what happened."

"There's still hope," she tells me.

My words are tight as I respond, "It's been two weeks."

Two weeks of not knowing what happened to him. First he was missing. Then the truck was found, but he wasn't. I'll never forget that moment. The terror that he was gone. But now… now we don't have any idea and the worst thoughts never leave me.

"I'm not okay," I confess into the phone and I barely hear her tell me that she's coming. To stay where I am. That it's going to be okay. I'm still holding the phone, hysterically crying when my front door barges open.

I wouldn't get through this without my friends.

But I don't know how I'll ever be okay unless they find him and he's okay.

Bennet is the love of my life and I know he's still here, I can feel it. It's not hope, it's knowing.

I love you, Bennet. Please come home to me.

◦

Bennet

I'm only vaguely aware of the movement around me but I don't want to be aware of it at all. I only want to dream of her. Their muffled voices call me Mister. Hands gently shake my shoulder. Sleep pulls me back though, with her beside me in our bed where I fell in love with her and her with me.

I'll wake up... I'll hold you again.
Until then... I'll have you in our dreams.

This is not the end…
The *Fall in Love Again* series will feature Bennet and Bree falling in love on the small fictional street of Cedar Lane over and over again while the real world has had other plans for them. Because love is endless and this is what forever means. In any and every life, their love was meant to be. And there's so much to tell in the dreams where they get to meet again for the first time every night.

There is more to come from the
Fall in Love Again series.

about the
Author

Thank you so much for reading my romances. I'm just a stay at home mom and avid reader turned author and I couldn't be happier.

I hope you love my books as much as I do!

More by Willow Winters
WWW.WILLOWWINTERSWRITES.COM/BOOKS

Made in the USA
Middletown, DE
31 October 2022